AGENT Amelia

Zombie Cows!

MICHAEL BROAD

Andersen Press
London

First published
in 2007 by
Andersen Press Limited,
20 Vauxhall Bridge Road,
London SW1V 2SA
www.andersenpress.co.uk

The right of Michael Broad to
be identified as the author and
illustrator of this work has been
asserted by him in accordance
with the Copyright, Designs and
Patents Act, 1988.

Mixed Sources
Product group from well-managed
forests and other controlled sources
www.fsc.org Cert no. TT-COC-2139
© 1996 Forest Stewardship Council

Printed and bound in Great Britain by
Cox & Wyman Ltd, Reading, Berkshire

Copyright
© Michael Broad, 2007
All rights reserved.

British Library Cataloguing in
Publication Data available.

ISBN 978 1 84270 663 3

For Cheryl

I'M AMELIA KIDD and I'm a secret agent.

Well, I'm not actually a secret agent. I don't work for the government or anything, but I've saved the world loads of times from evil geniuses and criminal masterminds. There are loads of them around if you know what to look for.

I'm really good at disguises. I make my own gadgets (which sometimes work), and I'm used to improvising in sticky situations – which you have to do all the time when you're a secret agent.

These are my Secret Agent Case Files.

The Case of the Zombie Cows

During the holidays, when Mum's not working, we go out for the day and usually try to go somewhere different each time. Most times we end up somewhere really cool, but other times we end up somewhere not so cool.

This time Mum decided on the local petting zoo. Which is cool if you're really young – but not so cool if you're a secret agent who has definitely grown out of fluffy bunny rabbits.

I admit I was in a bit of a sulk when we arrived, huffing and puffing as we made our way down the gravel path towards the farmyard. Unfortunately Mum saw this as an opportunity for a bit of interrogation.

'Amelia, why oh why do you insist on dragging that big heavy bag everywhere we go?' she said, jabbing a finger at my rucksack. 'I can't imagine what you think you'll need?'

'Stuff,' I said, eyeing her carefully over the top of my sunglasses.

Mum eyed me carefully back.

Sometimes saying 'stuff' will cover it and Mum won't bother to pursue the contents of my rucksack. But my mum is pretty smart and every so often curiosity gets the better of her.

'What kind of stuff exactly?' she asked.

'Drawing stuff,' I said innocently.

'So I can draw the
fluffy bunny
rabbits.'

Mum immediately raised a
suspicious eyebrow. I'd obviously gone
too far with the mention of fluffy
bunny rabbits; now I was going
to have to prove it or draw
unwanted attention to my
secret agent activities.

With the biggest sigh I could manage I heaved off my rucksack, unzipped the flap, pulled out a drawing book and a handful of pencils, and waved them in the air. Of course the rest of my bag was stuffed with secret agent stuff,

but in the last week I'd seen Mum grow increasingly inquisitive about my rucksack and had packed the book and pencils as a precaution.

You have to think ahead when you're a secret agent.

'I don't want to see them,' Mum shrugged innocently. 'I was just making conversation.'

As I suspected, the petting zoo wasn't very interesting.

The animals were cute but they were all small and fluffy, and I couldn't really see them anyway because there were lots of other kids crowding around – kids that were at least half my age!

To make matters worse Mum
bumped into an old friend and was
nattering for ages, so I sloped away to
look for some bigger, more grown-up
animals like horses or elephants. OK, I
didn't really expect to find an
elephant, but it was a farm so there
could be a horse.

I was in luck –
as soon as I
turned the
corner,

climbed a couple of fences and
negotiated my way through a hedge, I
eventually found the stables. But my
luck quickly ran out as
very loud voice stopped
me in my tracks.

'AMELIA KIDD!
WHAT ON EARTH
ARE *YOU* DOING
HERE?'

At first I thought Mum had seen me sneaking off, followed me and planned to march me back to the fluffy bunny rabbits. But then I realised the voice was much too high-pitched and whiny – which could mean only one other person.

I turned around slowly to see Trudy Hart storming across the courtyard in riding coat, boots and hat, and waving her crop at me.

Trudy is in my class at school and we don't get on, in fact we're sworn enemies.

'Well?' she demanded, eyeing me up and down with her nose high in the air.

Because she took me by surprise, I was about to explain that I was bored with the petting zoo and was looking for something more interesting to pet, but then I thought of a better response.

'It's none of your business!' I yelled.

'My daddy owns these stables so I think you'll find it is my business!' she snapped.

'Oh,' I said, lowering my voice and forcing my mouth into a fake smile. 'I wasn't doing any harm, I just wanted to see the horses.'

'They're not *rocking* horses, they're intelligent animals and I forbid you from going anywhere near them!'

Trudy sneered, and thrust
her riding crop in
the direction of
a nearby field.

'I will
allow you to
see the cows,
though, they're
awfully stupid so
you'll probably find you have a lot in
common!'

I was about to raise my voice
again when a short, thin man
appeared from one of the stables. My
secret agent senses immediately kicked
in when I noticed the man was
carrying a shiny black briefcase!

Evil
geniuses and
criminal
masterminds
often carry
briefcases to
hold their
fiendish plans
for world
domination.
That doesn't
mean *everyone*
who has a

briefcase is planning to take over the
world, but this man was obviously just
a stable hand, which made it *very*
suspicious.

'Lightning is ready for you, Miss
Trudy,' he said.

The man caught me peering at
him over my sunglasses and narrowed
his eyes, making him look like an
angry gnome. 'Is everything OK, Miss
Trudy?' he added cautiously.

'Yes, thank you, Albert,' said
Trudy, without looking round. 'It's just
one of those dreadful petting-zoo
people has got lost again, but I said
she could go and gawp at the cows.'

'But the cows aren't really part of—' Albert began, but Trudy cut him off.

'I *said* she could go and gawp at the cows,' Trudy repeated – pulling out her mobile phone and flicking it open in a threatening manner. 'Is there going to be a problem, Albert?'

'No, Miss,' he said hurriedly. 'No problem at all.'

Trudy
snapped
her
phone
shut and
grinned at
me.

'Off you
go then,' she
said, 'and if I catch
you near the stables
again, I'll have Albert run you off with
his pitchfork. Do you understand?'

I wasn't listening anymore, I was
watching Albert shuffling away and
looking very dodgy. Once he was out
of sight I turned my attention back to
Trudy; she was snorting through her
nostrils at being made to wait.

'Whatever,' I sighed, and casually strolled away.

I made my way towards the cow field and then hid behind the wall until Trudy finally trotted off on her horse. I planned to double back and carry out some stable surveillance – but first I needed a disguise.

Ducking into the empty cattle shed I rummaged through my rucksack.

Making room for the sketchbook and pencil decoy meant disguises were thin on the ground, so I had to make do with a plastic nose, moustache and glasses (all in one), and a flat cap. A glance in my compact mirror told me none of my flowery dresses would go with the moustache, but after a bit of snooping I found an old brown coat hanging in the shed.

Pulling the coat on over my rucksack to give myself a bit of a hunch, I stepped back into the yard and glanced around. I was about to head back for the stables when I heard a very strange sound coming from the field.

MOO-click-click!

MOO-click-click!

A small herd of cows were ambling awkwardly towards me, but there was something very odd about the way they moved, something creepy and clunky, like zombie cows.

The cows stopped suddenly
when they reached the fence and
peered at me through vacant eyes. I'd
never seen a cow up close before but I
was pretty sure they didn't tick – and
these cows were definitely ticking!

At first I thought they might be
time bombs made to look like cows,
but that didn't really make sense. So I
stood up on the fence, leaned over
and tapped one firmly on the head.
It was rock hard and echoed
like a tin drum, and on
closer inspection I
found that one
of the ears was
not an ear at
all but a large
metal key!

Slipping through the fence I gave the cow a quick once-over.

After a bit of expert tapping and knocking and banging, a small door clicked open in the cow's belly. Peering inside the hatch I found a mass of cogs and wheels and ratchets whirring around, which definitely explained the ticking.

The cow was made of clockwork!

Slamming the hatch I suddenly
noticed that none of the clockwork
cows actually had a tail, instead they
each had a radio-control antenna with
a tiny red beacon flashing at the end!

'Hmmm?' I thought to myself.

An antenna meant they were
not just clockwork cattle that roamed
the fields until their keys wound

down, which would be weird enough;
these cows were actually being
controlled by someone from a
distance!

Slowly
and discreetly
I pulled out
my compact
mirror, held it
up and
scanned
the scene
behind
me, and
there in the
stable courtyard was
Albert the shifty stable hand! He was
watching me closely while tapping
away frantically inside his briefcase.

Suddenly all the cows clicked
their heads in my direction.

'MOOOOO!' they boomed
together, and then started making
their way forward again. Dropping the
mirror I leaped back over the fence
just as the cows crashed through it!

Uh Oh!

In the courtyard Albert had
vanished around the back of the
stables so I ran after him as fast as my

disguise would allow – which was
faster than the cows, who were very
slow and ambled along like zombies.

Tucked away behind the stables
I found a chicken run and Albert was
standing behind the hutch with his
briefcase propped up against the roof.

I could now see that
it had an antenna
of its own
and was full
of dials and
buttons and
switches.

When he
saw me he gave
an evil-genius smile and prodded one
of the buttons dramatically.

Cluck-click-click!

Cluck-click-click!

With a whirring of tiny cogs
and wheels and ratchets every chicken
in the yard stopped acting like a
chicken and snapped
its head in my
direction.

They flapped their
wings angrily and
began bobbing up
and down like
demented pistons.

Glancing back around the stable
I could see the herd of cows were still
bumbling across the courtyard. It
wasn't exactly a stampede so I turned
my attention back to the chickens.

The bobbing seemed to be
powering up the springs in their legs
because one tin bird squatted down, a
click sounded, and then it launched
itself straight at me, snapping its beak
angrily.

Uh Oh!

Quick as a flash I grabbed a nearby shovel and volleyed the ball of flapping metal before it could peck my plastic nose off.

I'm quite good at tennis so it shot across the yard like a rocket, landing with a massive

CLANG!

The pecking projectiles whizzed through the air in rapid succession and I fended them off with my shovel. As the last of the clockwork chickens squatted, clicked and launched, I turned sideways and whacked it in the direction of a very angry Albert.

The tin torpedo sailed through the air and crashed into the briefcase knocking Albert off his feet.

The controls slid
down the roof of
the chicken coop
and Albert lunged
forward, but I was
quicker and
managed to
snatch it
midair.

'Give
that back!'
Albert
growled,
getting to
his feet
and dusting
himself off.

I knew Albert was short, but he
was a lot shorter than I'd realised.

In fact he was so short that I could keep the briefcase from his reach just by holding it up in the air. Albert looked even more like an angry gnome jumping up and down trying to grab the briefcase.

Eventually the little man tired himself out.

'Now, why don't you start by telling me what you're up to?' I demanded, and because I was taller I felt like a grown-up dealing with a naughty child.

'Are you planning to take over the world?'

'Uh?' said Albert, and seemed genuinely surprised. 'Of course not…'

'Then what?' I said, stepping back and peering inside the briefcase.

'I'm planning to take over the *horse racing* world!' he stated proudly.

'On a metal chicken?' I said, and then glanced back at the cows, who were now ambling around the corner and looking much more comical than scary. 'Or on one of those?' I added with a smirk.

'Oh, those are just experiments,' Albert said, shaking his head. 'Now I've perfected my mechanical-animal technology there isn't be a single horse that can beat Lightning.'

'Lightning?' I gasped. 'Trudy Hart's horse?'

'Lightning belongs to me!' snapped Albert. 'That little madam thinks she owns everything just because her father owns the stables, but he's mine – I made every cog and spring.'

'Lightning isn't even a real

horse?' I said, and was a little bit impressed.

'No, in fact he's *better* than a real horse!' said Albert, matter-of-factly.

Hearing the familiar tick-tick-ticking, I noticed that the herd had eventually caught up with me, so I scanned the control board inside the briefcase for the stop button.

It wasn't obvious what any of the buttons did, but in the centre was a big red one. Criminal masterminds and evil geniuses love big red buttons

in briefcases —
they usually mean
something bad like
an explosion or
an ejector seat
or something
like that.

But seeing as though Albert wasn't
technically trying to take over the
world I guessed that the big red
button just meant 'stop'.

So I pressed it.

That was when lots of things
happened all at once.

Albert leaped
forward yelling,

'NOOOOOOOOO!'

The slow stampede of
clockwork cows ground to a halt and
then each one exploded in a mass of
springs and cogs and little brass
wheels.

Moments later there was a very
loud shriek. It came from the
courtyard on the other side of the

stables and even in
all the chaos I knew
it belonged
to Trudy
Hart, because
I've heard her
shrieking loads of
times before.

'What have
you done?'
Albert groaned,
snatching the smoking briefcase and
clutching it to his chest.

'Er, I'm not sure,' I said
awkwardly. 'What *have* I done?'

'That was the *self-destruct* button,'
Albert sobbed, sinking helplessly to his
knees. 'It's linked to *all* the mechanical
animals and was there only for an

emergency, it was never supposed to be pressed!'

'Oh,' I said feebly. 'Sorry.'

I did feel bad for breaking Albert's animals, but then I decided it was probably best to put an end to his plot. If he'd succeeded in taking over the racing world, he would most likely have turned his attention to the rest of the world.

It's best to nip these things in the bud.

Leaving Albert with his briefcase,

I decided to make my way back
towards the petting zoo. Packing my
disguise away, I draped the brown coat
over the fence and stepped back
through the stables.

In the middle of the courtyard
sat a heap of clockwork, springs and

metal horse parts. In the middle of the
mechanical mess sat Trudy. She was
still perched in the saddle holding
onto the reins, angrily tapping the
hide with her riding crop.

'Giddy up!' she demanded, as
the metal torso creaked back and
forth.

'Nice rocking horse,' I said, slipping my sunglasses on with a smile.

The Case of the Perilous Pipe

'…so if you think about it, another day *really* won't make any difference,' I pleaded, standing outside the school gates with my hands clasped hopefully. 'I'm *already* a week behind.'

'And that's exactly why you need to go back today,' Mum said sternly.

'Your cold has gone and your temperature is back to normal, so there's really no reason to keep you away from school a moment longer.'

I coughed dramatically but Mum just rolled her eyes.

'Have a nice day!' she said, jumped back into the car and drove away.

I do like school, but I'd got used to sitting in bed watching TV and being waited on by Mum. It was also nice to have a break from being a secret agent and saving the world. I consoled myself with the fact that my first lesson of the day was music – something nice and relaxing to ease me back in.

Or so I thought!

In the week I'd been away our old music teacher had retired and had been replaced by someone called Mrs Piper. In my experience new teachers always spell trouble; they're usually quite clever and therefore prone to thoughts of world domination.

Admittedly the dodgy ones are mostly chemistry teachers or biology teachers, but even the odd maths teacher can be found calculating mathematical formulas to take over the world.

I'd never actually heard of a music teacher being a criminal mastermind or an evil genius, but I decided to keep an eye on Mrs Piper just in case.

In class, I peered over my sunglasses as the new music teacher took off her coat and arranged books on her desk, which wasn't at all suspicious.

Then, after calling the
register, she frowned
and ran her finger back
down the list of names.

'Amelia Kidd?'
she said, narrowing
her eyes.

'Here!' I said,
just in case she
was calling
the register
again.

'Yes, I know you're *here*,'
snapped Mrs Piper. 'But it seems
you were not *here* for my
first lesson last week.'

'I was sick,' I
said. 'But I'm pretty
sure I'll catch up.'

'I'm *absolutely certain* you will catch up!' said Mrs Piper firmly. 'Because when you return to this classroom at lunch time I will repeat the entire lesson to *ensure* you catch up!'

'Er…' I said, but she cut me off before I could come up with a decent excuse.

'Now, who can remind me of the wonderful tune we learned last week?' Mrs Piper demanded, closing the register and turning her attention to the rest of the class.

Every hand shot into the air and waved enthusiastically.

'Good,' she said, placing a long black case on her desk, flicking the clasp and pulling out a funny-looking recorder. 'Then you will have no trouble accompanying me on my medieval pipe.'

Mrs Piper played three notes and the class sang, 'La! La! La!'

Not knowing the tune or the point of the lesson, all I could do was watch and listen, which was much more difficult than it sounds. The class sang the same three notes over and over again like a broken record and the sound of the weird wooden instrument made my brain itch.

With each chorus of 'La! La! La!' my secret agent instincts told me something strange was going on in the classroom, but I couldn't put my finger on exactly what it was.

'La! La! La!'

To begin with everyone was very enthusiastic about the 'La! La! La!' No one was fidgeting or getting bored. Also, everyone sang exactly in time with the pipe which never happens with a bunch of kids singing together – unless they're in a choir, and even then…

I turned my attention to Mrs Piper, purse-lipped and shifting her fingers swiftly along the pipe. Then I looked at the instrument itself, which was intricately carved and looked very old, meaning it was probably an antique…

An antique!

'Aha!' I thought, because in my experience antiques are *always* trouble: whether they're cursed or enchanted or have spirits trapped in them, you can't trust antiques.

But could the whole class *really* be under the influence of the pipe?

The 'La! La! La!' ended abruptly and every head turned in my direction.

'Amelia Kidd!' snapped the teacher. 'Will you be joining in or do you plan to continue gazing around the room like a gormless frog?'

Being a secret agent means you have to think fast, and my fast thoughts told me I could now find out for certain if the class was under the influence of the strange antique pipe.

I glanced over to Trudy Hart.

Having just been singled out by the teacher *and* called a gormless frog, I knew Trudy couldn't resist a sneer or a snigger.

Trudy looked back and gave me a friendly smile, but it wasn't a sarcastic friendly smile, it was a *genuine* friendly smile that made the hairs on

the back of my neck
stand on end.

The class were
definitely under the
influence of the pipe!
Mrs Piper
played the same
tune once again and
the whole class sang it back
with perfect timing. She gave a
satisfied nod and then turned to me
with a raised eyebrow.

'La? La? La?' I

mumbled, uncertainly.

Mrs Piper
nodded again and was
about to resume playing
when the bell for
break time sounded.

Immediately the
whole class began
shifting and
fidgeting in their
chairs. It seemed
the bell had
broken the
trance, and for
confirmation of this
I turned to Trudy Hart.

   She immediately screwed up her
nose and poked her tongue out at me.

At break time I was sitting on a
bench, trying to work out how to get
a closer look at Mrs Piper's peculiar
pipe, when the din from the
playground was suddenly replaced by
an eerie silence.

I looked around over my sunglasses.

All the kids had mysteriously stopped playing, running and screaming and stood perfectly still like statues. Then I heard a familiar tune coming from the window of the music room and saw the silhouette of Mrs Piper and her pipe.

'La! La! La!'   'La! La! La!'

Singing the song of the distant pipe, the whole playground turned to face me and began walking in my direction, and not just the kids from *my* music class, it was every kid in the school.

Everyone except me was under Mrs Piper's spell!

Realising the music teacher was on to me I grabbed my rucksack and was about to leg it when another sound echoed through the playground – the bell signalling the end of break time.

All the kids
stopped, looked
around and began
scratching their
heads.

The bell had broken the spell
again, but it was too close for comfort.
Pulling on my rucksack, I hurried back
into school and ran straight to the next
class on my timetable.

It was computer studies, and I
had some research to do!

After a week away from school, I knew I'd be a bit behind on most of my subjects, but computer studies wasn't one of them. Secret agents have to be super quick on computers so I'm always ahead of everyone else – and I planned to use that time to find out about medieval pipes and the mysterious Mrs Piper.

It took me a while, but after a lot of digging I found a picture of Mrs Piper's pipe. It was called the Perilous Pipe and loads of historical documents mentioned it. As I suspected the instrument was enchanted, which means a spell had been cast on it back in the days when people cast spells.

The Perilous Pipe had been enchanted nearly three hundred years ago – or rather the reed that makes the sound *inside* the pipe had been enchanted – but what was interesting was that it had originally belonged to someone called The Piper!

Which was all a bit too much of a coincidence if you ask me.

I made another search.

There were lots of different references to The Piper, some were stories and others were real historical accounts from old newspapers and journals. The one thing they all had in common was what The Piper was famous for.

He was famous for leading children away using the Perilous Pipe!

I even found an old-fashioned drawing of The Piper and the resemblance made me gasp out loud.

I glanced up from
the screen to make sure
no one had heard me
and I was just in
time to see Mrs
Piper creeping past
the window with a large
pair of bolt cutters!

This made me
gasp even louder!

'Amelia?' said Mr
Moore. 'Are you feeling well?'

The tech
teacher looked
concerned and
started weaving
through the
computer desks
towards me.

Thinking fast I quickly cleared the
screen and pulled a big wad of tissues
out of my rucksack.

I wiped my
nose and peered
helplessly up
at him.

'Just a few sniffles!' I sighed,
glancing sideways at the clock.

It was ten minutes to lunch time
and I decided I could use those ten
minutes to snoop around Mrs Piper's

classroom. Taking a deep breath I launched an enormous coughing fit into my tissues.

'Oh, dear!' said Mr Moore. 'I think you should take yourself along to see the nurse immediately.'

Pulling on my rucksack I nodded bravely and headed for the door, throwing in a couple of sniffs for good measure. Once out of sight I pocketed the tissues and bolted.

Backing along the wall of the corridor I peered through the door of the music room – there were no lessons going on inside but Mrs Piper had already returned. She was standing at the window looking out into the playground where I'd seen her at break time.

On her desk lay the Perilous Pipe.

This was my chance!

Opening the door quietly, I crept into the classroom and tiptoed towards the desk, but I'd only made it halfway before Mrs Piper spoke, and because it startled me I froze to the spot.

'The mark of a truly gifted musician is excellent hearing,' said Mrs Piper, turning round dramatically and glancing at her watch. 'You're early!'

I smiled innocently and shrugged.

Mrs Piper narrowed her eyes.

'*Why* are you early?' she added suspiciously.

Our eyes met over the Perilous Pipe and as the expression on Mrs Piper's face changed I realised she'd rumbled me. We both ran for the pipe at the same time, but as Mrs Piper was much taller, I knew she'd get there first.

I reached into my pocket, hoping I'd left a small gadget there or *something* I could use to even the odds, but what I found was the wad of paper tissues.

Not ideal, but I threw them at her anyway.

'URRRRGGGH!' she
shrieked, batting the air angrily as the
tissue-storm surrounded her – the
tissues were actually clean, but Mrs

Piper didn't know that. I quickly scrabbled onto the desk and searched for the pipe, but as the last of the tissues fluttered down I saw that it was gone.

'Looking for this?' smiled Mrs Piper, waving the weird wooden instrument in the air triumphantly.

'You won't get away with it!' I said angrily.

'Oh, don't bother trying to get me to rant about my plans,' she said dismissively. 'I'm going to steal all the children away with my pipe and then hold the world to ransom. It's that simple really.'

I'd never met an evil genius or a criminal mastermind that didn't like ranting about their evil plans, so this took me by surprise.

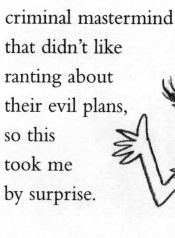

The taking-over-the-world rant usually gives me time to come up with a strategy, but Mrs Piper didn't hang around.

She lifted the pipe to her lips and began playing.

I still hadn't been brainwashed by the tune, but as the sound filtered out of the classroom I heard chairs scraping across the floor all over the school, followed by the sound of footsteps marching towards the music room.

Soon the corridor outside filled
with kids and Trudy Hart was right at
the front wearing that creepy friendly
smile.

My only chance for escape was
the lunch time bell breaking the spell.
I looked at the clock and saw more
than ten minutes had passed since
leaving the computer room.

The bell should have sounded
already!

'Ring! Ring! It's lunch time!' sang Mrs Piper. 'And now I think it's time for you to catch up with the rest of your class,' she added, shifting her fingers along the pipe and pursing her lips.

Now I knew what Mrs Piper had been doing with the bolt cutters! Seeing the flaw in her plan at break time she'd crept around the school and disconnected all the bells.

I looked around frantically for an escape route, but the kids were blocking the door and the windows were too high up. I tried to remember our last fire drill and whether there was an emergency exit somewhere nearby…

Fire drill! I thought, tipping my sunglasses and smiling at Mrs Piper.

My smile obviously took her by surprise because she paused for a moment, and in that moment I snatched the Perilous Pipe, whacked it against the fire alarm and legged it for the door.

As the sound of the fire bells filled the corridor, the kids began scratching their heads, and as I barged past Trudy I was relieved to see her poking her tongue out at me.

Confused teachers were flapping their arms amid the sea of equally confused kids, trying to organise everyone for the fire drill, and in all the chaos no one noticed as I ducked down and rummaged in my rucksack.

Tucking my hair
up inside a
baseball cap
I quickly
blended back
into the crowd as we

were led outside to form orderly lines.

I kept my head down and the
pipe behind my back as Mrs Piper
stalked the lines of kids – and she
walked straight past me twice thinking
I was just one of many boys in
baseball caps.

When the fire alarm was re-set the teachers spread out and began calling the registers. Peering under the peak of my cap I saw Mrs Piper abandon her search and smile to herself as the names were called.

As 'K' for 'Kidd' drew nearer on the register I wracked my brains, thinking about the research and the stories and the enchantment… Aha! I thought, blindly fiddling with the pipe behind my back.

'Amelia Kidd?' called Mr Moore.

'Here!' I said, slipping off the baseball cap.

Mrs Piper leaped forward, shoved Mr Moore out of the way and snatched the pipe from behind my back.

'You fool!' she yelled, jabbing the antique instrument in my direction like a duelling sword. 'You thought you could prevent *me* from taking over the world?'

'Excuse me?' said Mr Moore, frowning at Mrs Piper.

'Yes, you heard me correctly,'
snapped the music teacher. 'I plan to
take over the world. It is a genius plan
involving my enchanted pipe…'

It seemed Mrs Piper couldn't
resist a rant after all, and she ranted on
and on and on, revealing every aspect
of her plot for world domination.

It was actually one of the longest rants I've ever heard from an evil genius or criminal mastermind.

Of course everyone was looking at Mrs Piper as though she'd gone mad, especially when she lifted the pipe to her lips, positioned her hands over the appropriate holes and blew…

… and no sound came out.

There was a scuffle when Mrs
Piper lunged for me, but she was
quickly restrained and taken away,
yelling about interfering little
hooligans, and magical pipes, and
stolen enchanted reeds.

A few kids giggled and the teachers shook their heads sadly.

When Mum picked me up she asked if I'd missed anything interesting during my week off sick. Pulling the enchanted reed from my back pocket, I tipped my glasses and studied it closely. It was obviously harmless without the pipe so I snapped it in half and flicked the pieces out of the window.

'Not really,' I said, smiling to myself. 'But it's *definitely* good to be back.'

The Case of the Creepy Cakes

On Saturdays Mum takes me to the cake shop around the corner and we treat ourselves to a jam doughnut or a fresh cream cake. We've done it for as long as I can remember and I always look forward to it.

Or at least I *used* to look forward to it…

In the week since our last visit the cake shop had mysteriously closed

down and re-opened calling itself
'The Beauty Sisters' Cake Emporium',
which is a bit of a flashy name for a
cake shop if you ask me.

But the shop wasn't the only
thing that was different.

'Look at the size of those
doughnuts!' Mum squealed as we
passed the window of the shop.

'They must be twice the size of the old ones, and they're half the price too!' she gasped.

I tipped my glasses and peered at the selection of cakes.

It was true, the doughnuts were massive – in fact all the cakes in the window were freakishly huge. There were enormous éclairs, colossal cream horns, mammoth meringues – and all at half the regular price.

My first instinct was to get excited like Mum had, but then my secret agent instincts kicked in and I viewed the outsized cakes with suspicion. I wanted to know *why* the cakes were so big, *why* they were so cheap, and *who* were the strangely generous Beauty Sisters?

Because evil
geniuses and criminal
masterminds don't
usually hang out in
cake shops I hadn't
brought my rucksack
full of gadgets. But I

still had my sunglasses, so I adjusted
them carefully to conceal my identity
and slipped discreetly into the shop.

Any hope of going unnoticed while carrying out preliminary surveillance was foiled when Mum entered the shop behind me clapping her hands together loudly.

'I THINK I'VE JUST DIED AND GONE TO HEAVEN!' she shrieked, gazing with wide eyes at wall-to-wall shelves stuffed with every confection known to man.

Behind the counter, the heads of
two thin figures snapped in our
direction. For a fraction of a second
the elderly pair narrowed their eyes,
but then they quickly stretched their
mouths into wide friendly smiles.

'Welcome to The Beauty Sisters'
Cake Emporium!' they sang, ignoring
me to focus their greeting on Mum.

Which was handy, because now I had a chance to size them up without drawing attention to myself.

The first remarkable thing about the Beauty Sisters was that they were identical twins. Everything about them was a mirror image and probably had been for about a hundred years because they both looked ancient.

The second remarkable thing was how they were dressed.

As they stepped out from behind the counter the pair were both unbelievably glamorous – but it wasn't the usual funky-grandma kind of glamour. This was full-on catwalk glamour, complete with mad clothes, huge hairdos and tonnes of bright make-up.

Mum's wide eyes grew a little wider when confronted with the Beauty Sisters, so much so that for a moment she seemed unable to speak.

'Goodness me,' she gasped eventually. 'You're both, er...'

'Beautiful?' the sisters chimed together. 'Yes, we know.'

'Um, yes!' Mum stammered. 'That's *exactly* what I was about to say!'

'We used to be supermodels, you know,' the pair stated proudly.

While the grown-ups made small talk I scanned the shop for signs of criminal activity. But aside from the size of the cakes there was nothing out of the ordinary, except for the peculiar-looking twins.

'...and however do you both stay so slim?' Mum laughed. 'If I had a shop like this I'd be tempted to eat cakes all day long,' she added, and then laughed some more.

The twins were not laughing at Mum's joke. In fact they'd stopped smiling altogether and their identical faces suddenly wore the same grave expression.

'We *never* eat the cakes,' they hissed, and with this the sisters hurried

back behind the counter and busied
themselves behind a display of giant
French Fancies.

'Oh,' said Mum, to fill the
awkward silence.

While Mum tried to work out
what she'd said wrong, I crept over
to the counter. Tipping my sunglasses,

I watched as the angry twins
whispered to each other while
frantically tying pink bows around
bags of marzipan sweets.

Suddenly two pairs of eyes
glared in my direction.

'What do you want, little girl?'
they said in unison.

'Two doughnuts, please!' I said,
and did my best innocent smile.

Back home
I eyed the bag of
doughnuts on the
kitchen counter.
They did look and
smell delicious, but
I didn't plan on
Mum or me
eating them. The

Beauty Sisters were up to something –
probably trying to take over the world
– and I was certain the cakes were at
the bottom of it.

I studied the contents of the
paper bag and wondered what an evil
genius or a criminal mastermind
could possibly do with a doughnut,
and the answer seemed pretty obvious
to me.

Holding the bag at arm's length I gripped each doughy ball through the paper and began a slow, controlled squeeze. Then, with my face still screwed up because I half-expected the doughnuts to explode, I peered into the bag and was a bit disappointed to see two saggy doughnuts and a bag full of jam.

Hmmm?

I dipped my finger in the sticky red goo and held it up to my nose. It smelled OK but I still didn't want to eat it. Instead, I pulled out my magnifying glass and moved to the window for a closer look.

It was then that something strange happened: as the heat from the sun intensified through the magnifying glass, the jam started bubbling and expanding right before my eyes!

'Heat!' I gasped.

I flicked the red blob away, grabbed the doughnut bag and plonked it on the hot radiator. The jam in the bag immediately began to swell. It strained at the paper and then rose up out the top like a soufflé. Thinking fast I ran to the bin and threw the whole thing in just as the paper burst and spilled the red mess everywhere.

'What on earth?' yelled Mum, appearing in the doorway.

'Er, I dropped our doughnuts in the bin… *accidentally*,' I stammered, although given more time I would definitely have come up with a better excuse.

Mum gazed at the red mess in the bin.

'And they look like really jammy ones too,' she sighed.

'I'll run back to the shop!' I said quickly. 'My treat!' And before Mum could answer I grabbed my rucksack and bolted for the door. Round the corner, I stopped and had a rummage. Without time to prepare, I wasn't sure what disguises I'd packed and all I could find was a beret and a flowery scarf that I'd collected because I might need to look like a French lady one day.

It was not ideal, but it would have to do.

Walking slowly past the window of the cake shop I spied the Beauty Sisters. They were busy talking to customers at the counter so I seized the opportunity to slip into the shop. Once inside, I edged my way discreetly along the wall pretending to browse the shelves, while secretly heading for a curtain at the back.

With one last glance to make sure the twins were still distracted, I was about to duck through the curtain when a terrifying noise stopped me in my tracks.

'BUT I WANT IT NOOOOOW!' screamed a strangely familiar voice.

I froze to the spot.

Pulling my beret down and my scarf up, I turned my head again slowly to find the customers in the shop were actually my archenemy, Trudy Hart, and her weary-looking parents.

Trudy is in my class at school but we don't get on. She's very spoiled and used to getting her own way. Today, that meant screaming and stamping her foot in the middle of the shop while her parents tried to calm her down.

Typical! I thought.

Then I realised that with Trudy in a full-on tantrum, everyone's attention was focused on her and no one was looking at me. So I shrugged my shoulders and stepped casually through the curtain.

I'd never seen the back of a cake shop before so I didn't really know what to expect, but I definitely didn't expect to find what I found. The back of The Beauty Sisters' Cake Emporium looked exactly like a mad scientist's laboratory!

There were test tubes and lightning rods and smoking beakers, and among all the complicated scientific equipment were bags of sugar, sacks of flour, pots of cream and jars of jam. There was also a light frost covering everything because the room was as cold as a freezer.

Hmmm? I thought, rubbing my arms for warmth.

My plan to get into the back of the shop didn't really cover what I would do once I got there, so I decided to snoop around a bit and hope I'd discover exactly what the Beauty Sisters were plotting.

Then I'd find a way to stop them.

I could hear Trudy still screaming her demands in the shop and, knowing she would continue to scream until she got her own way, I set about a thorough search of the weird cake laboratory.

Starting with the diagrams on the wall.

As far as I could work out from the drawings, the twins were filling their cakes with specially modified

fillings that would instantly make
people gain weight – which was odd.
I'd foiled some strange attempts to
take over the world before, but this
was definitely one of the strangest.

I also worked out from the
diagrams that body heat triggered the
swelling of the fillings, which
explained why my tampering
with the doughnuts had set
off the weird expanding
jam, but as bodies aren't
as hot as radiators, people
probably wouldn't
explode.

They would just get very, very big!

Scattered around the room were large crates filled with cakes and buns, but it was so cold in the lab I decided they were probably harmless so long as I didn't eat them or warm them up. Then I noticed a table in the middle of the room with a large cotton cloth draped over it.

There was no way of knowing
what was underneath and it could
have been a booby trap, so I pulled
out my extendable grabber-hand
gadget (which is basically a hand on a
stick) and carefully removed the cloth.

Underneath the cloth was the
biggest Victoria Sponge I'd ever seen!
It was about half my size and stuffed
to bursting with jam and cream. Then
I peered down at the cake and gasped
out loud.

The words 'Happy Birthday Trudy' glared back at me in bright pink icing!

I could have kicked myself for not making the connection earlier.

Trudy had made a big fuss all week at school about her birthday party – she even held a meeting in the playground where the exclusive party invitations were handed out, along with a typed list of acceptable birthday presents.

Needless to say I didn't get an invitation – and now I was staring at her birthday cake.

Suddenly everything went eerily silent and I realised the sound of Trudy screaming and stamping had stopped. Which could mean only one thing. Either Trudy had just got her own way, or she'd left the shop quietly *without* getting her own way.

I knew Trudy well enough to know which was most likely and turned round to find two thin figures looming in the doorway!

'Er… *bonjour!*' I said quickly, in my best French accent. '*Croissants?*' I added hopefully, having just exhausted my entire French vocabulary.

The twins eyed me up and
down and then scuttled forwards.

'You're not French,' said the twin on the left.

'You're not chic enough,' added the twin on the right.

I backed away slowly and tried to think fast.

One sure way to buy time with criminal masterminds is to get them ranting about their plans for world domination – most of them can't resist telling you how clever they think they are.

'You won't get away with it!' I said, which is usually a good trigger.

The twins stopped and frowned at each other; the pair had seen right through my disguise so perhaps they were too smart to fall for the rant-trigger, and having backed myself into the corner of the room I could only wait and hold my breath.

'We WILL get away with it!'
they yelled in unison. 'Once the world
gets a taste of our delicious cakes
they'll all puff up like marshmallows,
and soon EVERYONE will be a big
roly-poly dumpling…'

While the Beauty Sisters
continued to rant I looked around
frantically. The twins were blocking
the door so there was no way out –

which meant I had to cause a
diversion to get past them.

My eyes fell on the thermostat
mounted on the wall beside me.

'Aha!' I said to myself, because if
I said it out
loud it would
completely
give the game
away. Aiming
carefully I
flicked the
lever on my
extendable
grabber-
hand and

spun the dial from 'Arctic' to
'Tropical', then tucked the gadget
away again in the blink of an eye.

'…and when everyone else is waddling around like great big balloons, WE will be the only THIN ones. Then the fashion world will have no choice but to make us supermodels again!' concluded the Beauty Sisters.

'Not bad,' I said, and I said it out loud because I needed to buy more time. 'Except for one tiny flaw,' I added, casually loosening my scarf because the room was already heating up.

'What flaw?' asked the twins suspiciously. 'Our plan is flawless, like us!'

'You didn't count on *me* stopping you!' I said firmly.

Suddenly a cream horn exploded in the corner of the room,

splurting its filling right
across the ceiling,
followed by another, and
another. Then whole trays of
doughnuts and cream cakes started
blowing up all over the place.

BANG!

BANG!

BANG!

SPLAT! SPLAT! SPLAT!

The twins gripped each other and shrieked with each explosion, while I cloaked myself in the cotton cloth and headed for the door, ducking and diving through the minefield of flying fillings.

I was halfway to freedom when the explosions suddenly stopped, and all that remained was the foaming fillings, flowing from the trays.

The angry twins lunged forward but I ducked behind the table in the middle of the room.

Now the only thing that stood between the twins and me was the giant Victoria Sponge. Glancing down I saw that it was already beginning to throb, and the Beauty Sisters had seen it too because they were backing away.

Thinking on my feet I grabbed the giant cake, heaved it above my head and took off after them, which was difficult because it was really heavy.

Then as soon as I was close enough I lobbed the cake as hard as I could.

I watched in slow motion as the cake sailed through the air, but the twins were quick and managed to duck down just in time. The giant cake flew over their heads, through the curtain and out into the shop.

BANG! SPLAT!

The explosion made the curtain
flap inwards and through the gap I
saw a Trudy-shaped pillar of jam
and cream with a sponge on top.

This was quickly followed by an ear-
piercing squeal that made the
windows rattle.

Trudy did look funny covered in
cake, but there was no time to enjoy
it. The twins had picked themselves up
and now looked even meaner than
before. I glanced around frantically
and grabbed the nearest things to
hand.

Two squeezy bags of bright pink
icing!

With an expert flick of my wrists I cocked the icing bags and aimed them steadily at the twins. The Beauty Sisters immediately put their hands up in surrender – which was just as well because that's when Trudy's parents appeared through the curtain, keen to know why their daughter was buried under a giant cake.

When you're a secret agent you can't hang around and take credit for saving the world, and because all the evidence was there in the cake-lab I quickly armed Mr and Mrs Hart with the icing bags and made my getaway.

I couldn't risk revealing my identity as I passed the creamy, jammy mountain in the middle of the shop. But as two furious eyes peered out at me, I couldn't resist a quick comment either.

'*Bonjour, croissant!*' I said, in my best French accent, and then legged it.

Watch out for my other book

AGENTAmelia Ghost Diamond!

Three more
fabulously funny
stories

AGENT AMELIA: Ghost Diamond   ISBN 9781842706626   £4.99